Turkey's Escape Plan

Written by
Julia Zheng

Illustrated by
Nurul Ashari

Copyright © 2022 Qinghong Zheng

First printing edition, 2022
Library of Congress Control Number: 2022906225
ISBN: 979-8-9860451-3-9

Printed in the United States of America

For my family with love

Turkey was a new resident of Cranberry Farm. Recently, he had been very worried. Thanksgiving was approaching, and the rumor was that Turkey would be a dish for dinner!

All the animals on the farm wanted to do something nice for Turkey before Mr. and Mrs. Woods took him away.

Cow sent him milk every day.

Chicken sent him corn.

Sheep sent him flowers.

Turkey sat on a pile of hay and wondered what he could do to escape. A few ideas came to him.

Turkey went to Swan. "Hi, Swan. Can you please teach me how to fly? I've got an escape plan. Maybe I can fly away once I learn how!"

"Sure," said Swan, and she started to show Turkey how her wings flutter.

Turkey did the same, but his body stayed on the ground no matter how hard he tried.

"Never mind," Turkey sighed. "I don't think this is a good idea. My wings are just not strong enough to lift my body!"

The next day, Turkey went to Rabbit. "Hi, Rabbit. Can you please teach me how to dig a deep hole? I've got an escape plan. Maybe I can dig a hole to get away!"

"Sure," said Rabbit, and she started to show Turkey how to dig a hole.

Turkey did the same, but his legs quickly got tired.

"Never mind," Turkey sighed. "This is not going to work! I will never have enough time to dig a hole that goes outside this farm before Thanksgiving."

On the third day, Turkey went to Horse. "Hi, Horse. Can you please teach me how to run really fast? I've got an escape plan. Maybe I can run so fast that Mr. and Mrs. Woods won't be able to catch me!"

"Sure," said Horse, and he started to show Turkey how to run fast by using all the strength in his legs. But no matter how hard Turkey moved his legs, he just could not catch up to Horse. "Never mind," Turkey panted. "This is impossible for me! I don't think my legs are strong enough to run fast like you."

Turkey was very sad the night before Thanksgiving. He wrote a letter to all his friends on the farm, telling them how thankful he was for their friendship.

Thanksgiving was here, and Turkey was extremely nervous! He waited anxiously for Mr. and Mrs. Woods to come and take him. Finally, Mrs. Woods came. Turkey closed his eyes. But to his surprise, Mrs. Woods gave him some extra food and said with a smile, "Happy Thanksgiving, Turkey!"

Turkey waited all day, but nothing bad happened. He was confused! So, he went to the house to see what was going on.

Turkey looked through the window and saw Mr. and Mrs. Woods sitting at a table, praying. Their Thanksgiving meal was a whole stuffed, roasted pumpkin with pumpkin pie for dessert.

It dawned on Turkey that both Mr. and Mrs. Woods were, in fact, vegetarians!

Turkey laughed to himself. "How silly have I been? All my worries were for nothing! It's a happy Thanksgiving, after all. I sure feel thankful!"

About the Author

Julia Zheng is a children's author from Fujian, China. She now lives in Massachusetts. Zheng graduated from Nanchang University, where she majored in English and studied Western culture. She taught English in a primary school in southern China before moving to the United States. Her teaching experience and passion  for writing have inspired her to write children's books, especially stories that convey important messages through humor, warmth, and a happy or unexpected ending.

For more books by Julia Zheng, please visit her Amazon Author Page: https://www.amazon.com/author/juliazheng

Other books by Julia Zheng available on Amazon:

Made in the USA
Coppell, TX
16 November 2024

40366326R00017